The
Tiara
Club

Also in the Tiara Club

VIVIAN FRENCH

The Tiara Club

Princess Emily
AND THE
Substitute Fairy

ILLUSTRATED BY SARAH GIBB

KATHERINE TEGEN BOOKS
An Imprint of HarperCollins*Publishers*

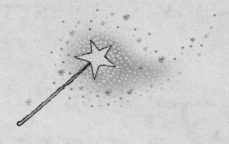

Library of Congress Cataloging-in-Publication Data
French, Vivian.
  Princess Emily and the substitute fairy / by Vivian French ;
illustrated by Sarah Gibb. — 1st U.S. ed.
    p. cm. — (The Tiara Club)
  Summary: After substitute Fairy Angora's wishes go awry,
Princess Emily helps to bring Fairy G. back to the Academy to
fix the problems.
  ISBN-10: 0-06-112436-2 — ISBN-13: 978-0-06-112436-5
  [1. Princesses—Fiction. 2. Wishes—Fiction. 3. Magic—
Fiction. 4. Schools—Fiction.] I. Gibb, Sarah, ill. II. Title.
PZ7.F88917Prie 2007   2006036261
[Fic]—dc22   CIP
                                                     AC

Typography by Amy Ryan
❖
First U.S. edition, 2007

For Princess Emily of Edinburgh,
with much love
—V.F.

For the little princesses: Abi, Georgie,
Joesie, Tabi, Imi, and Freya
—S.G.

The Royal Palace Academy
for the Preparation of Perfect Princesses
(Known to our students as "The Princess Academy")

OUR SCHOOL MOTTO:
A Perfect Princess always thinks of others before herself, and is kind, caring, and truthful.

We offer the complete curriculum for all princesses, including:

How to Talk to a Dragon

Creative Cooking for Perfect Palace Parties

Wishes, and How to Use Them Wisely

Designing and Creating the Perfect Ball Gown

Avoiding Magical Mistakes

Descending a Staircase as if Floating on Air

Our principal, Queen Gloriana, is present at all times, and students are in the excellent care of the school Fairy Godmother.

VISITING TUTORS AND EXPERTS INCLUDE:

KING PERCIVAL *(Dragons)*

LADY VICTORIA *(Banquets)*

QUEEN MOTHER MATILDA *(Etiquette, Posture, and Poise)*

THE GRAND HIGH DUCHESS DELIA *(Fashion)*

We award tiara points to encourage
our princesses toward the next level.
Each princess who earns enough points
in her first year is welcomed to the
Tiara Club and presented with a silver tiara.

Tiara Club princesses are invited to return
next year to Silver Towers, our very special
residence for Perfect Princesses, where they
may continue their education at a higher level.

PLEASE NOTE:

Princesses are expected to arrive
at the Academy with a *minimum* of:

TWENTY BALL GOWNS
*(with all necessary hoops,
petticoats, etc.)*

TWELVE DAY-DRESSES

SEVEN GOWNS
*suitable for garden parties
and other special daytime
occasions*

TWELVE TIARAS

DANCING SHOES
five pairs

VELVET SLIPPERS
three pairs

RIDING BOOTS
two pairs

*Cloaks, muffs, stoles, gloves,
and other essential
accessories, as required*

Hi there! I'm Princess Emily—one of the Rose Room Princesses from the Princess Academy. Do you know Alice, and Katie, and Daisy, and Charlotte, and Sophia? They're my best friends—just like you! And have you met Princess Perfecta yet? She's awful. Alice says it's because some people are just born that way—they can't help being nasty.

All the same, I wish Perfecta wasn't in our class. But at least I have my best friends—and you!

Chapter One

$\mathcal{D}$o you ever feel like there is a big black cloud hanging over your head? Well, the day after my birthday was like that. Isn't that awful? Even though my parents had sent me the most completely gorgeous pearly pink dress and a perfect matching tiara, I didn't feel excited.

All of us in the Rose Room had been worrying for weeks about what we were going to wear for the Grand Assembly at the end of term, so it was very nice of my parents to send me something so utterly beautiful—but it meant I'd

be different from my very best friends. That made me feel terrible! They'd all raved about my beautiful gown, of course, but I knew that secretly it *must* have made them feel bad.

I'd opened my package at breakfast, and I couldn't help noticing the tiny pause before they

told me how pretty it was.

And then Princess Perfecta said in a *really* nasty voice, "Who's going to be the biggest show-off on Saturday?" And Princess Floreen said, "*Some* people are just spoiled!"

But that wasn't the only reason for my big black cloud. I was worried about my tiara points. Honestly, I was worried sick.

"I just *know* I'm going to be here in first year for ever and ever and ever," I said as I stood staring out of the Recreation Room window.

"Me too." Princess Katie sighed. She came over to stand beside me. "I got five minus points yesterday. I went down to the stable to see the ponies that pull the silver coach, and I forgot to wipe my boots when I came back in. Queen Mother Matilda gave me a terrible scolding."

"You did have a lot of straw in your hair too," Princess Sophia pointed out.

"*And* you took all the sugar cubes from the tea service," Princess Alice said. "Perfecta was furious!"

"Serves her right," said Princess Charlotte. She gave me a comforting smile. "Please stop worrying, Emily. You must have more tiara points than Perfecta and Floreen."

"But do any of us have enough to join the Tiara Club?" Princess Daisy asked. Nobody answered.

We couldn't, because we really and truly had no idea. We were meant to keep track of our tiara points in our diaries, but we were always forgetting! And even when we *did* remember, we often added

them up all wrong. (Especially me.) Up until now, we'd just hoped for the best, but all of a sudden it was serious!

The Grand Assembly was the most important day of our lives, because that's the day when we'd find out if we'd earned our places in the Tiara Club. And it was only two days away! It was very scary!

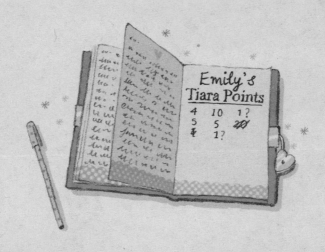

"Maybe," Alice said hopefully, "we could ask Fairy G. how many points we've got?"

Charlotte made a face. "She won't say. I asked her the other day."

"She just said Perfect Princesses don't need to worry." Katie sighed again.

"What if we asked if we need to do just a *little* bit better or a *lot* better?" I suggested.

Daisy shook her head. "We can't! She's in bed with a horrible cold."

"Can't she magic it away?" I asked.

"I don't think she can use magic

on herself," Sophia said. "She can only—"

Crash!

The Recreation Room door flung open, and Princess Jemima came zooming in, her eyes wide.

"Have you *heard*?" she gasped.
"Fairy G.'s going away!"

We stared at her.

"What do you mean?" I asked.

"She's been so sick that Queen
Gloriana's sending her off to stay

with one of her sisters—Fairy G.'s sisters, that is, not Queen Gloriana's. And we've got a substitute teacher instead, and she's called Fairy Angora!" Jemima stopped to take a breath. "Queen Gloriana says we all have to go to the Great Hall to meet her, so you've got to come *now*!" And she shot off at high speed.

We looked at one another in astonishment. Apart from Queen Gloriana, Fairy G. is the *most* important person at the Princess Academy. She's the one who takes care of us and tucks us in to bed at night. She teaches many of our lessons as well. She's really fun, even if she does swell up in a big way when she's angry! Queen Gloriana is okay, but she can be a bit scary.

I don't know about the others, but I felt quite shaky. It was almost like when I'm at home and my mom has to go off for a Royal Tour, and I get left behind.

"I do hope she gets better soon," I said. Charlotte nodded.

"Do you think she'll be better by the end of term?" Sophia asked.

"If she isn't," Daisy said, "who'll tell us about our tiara points?"

Alice shrugged. "Queen Gloriana,

I guess. Come on! Let's go and check out—what was her name?"

"Fairy Angora," Katie said, and we trooped out of the Recreation Room and along the black-and-white marble corridor that leads to the Great Hall. As we came through the door, Queen Gloriana was walking onto the stage, and beside her was the most *beautiful* fairy!

Chapter Two

I don't think any of us heard what Queen Gloriana said for at least the first two minutes. We were all too busy staring. Fairy Angora was so lovely, and her dress was totally *amazing*. It was made of some strange shimmery material, and it kept changing color. First it was soft pink, and then pale blue . . . and then it drifted back to pink again. I suddenly realized Queen Gloriana was still talking.

". . . and *so*, Princesses," she said, "as the Fairy Godmother Agency is extremely short-staffed, Fairy Angora has agreed to come, even though she has not quite completed her training yet. And now, please give Fairy Angora a *huge* welcome to the Princess Academy!" Of course we all clapped wildly.

As we moved out of the Great Hall there was a massive buzz of excitement. Fairy G. usually gave the next lesson, How to Avoid Magical Mistakes, so maybe we'd have Fairy Angora now instead!

We practically ran to the class-room. As we pulled out our chairs,

there was a tinkling noise, and
Fairy Angora floated in.

"Ooooooh," she said, and her
voice was small and sweet and
whispery. "Aren't you all so charm-
ing? Now, what shall we do first?"

She looked around. "Oh, dear. So boring! Shall we make this a *pretty* room?" She waved her wand. Silver sparkles flew in all directions—and the next minute there were roses everywhere!

Perfecta raised her hand. "Excuse me," she said, "but that was amazing! What else can you do?"

Fairy Angora blushed. "Oh, quite a lot of things, really. Of course, I'm not quite up to pumpkins and coaches. That's next term."

Perfecta smiled a very fake smile. "So," she said, "do you know about wishes?"

"Oh, yes!" Fairy Angora beamed. "I know *all* about wishes!"

And then—would you believe it? Perfecta burst into absolute floods of tears and sobbed. "That's so *wonderful*! Please, please, *please* can I have a wish? I have *nothing* to wear for the Grand Assembly!"

Princess Perfecta is very clever. We all knew she wasn't really crying, but enormous tears streamed down her cheeks as she gazed imploringly at our substitute teacher.

Fairy Angora hesitated. "Well . . ." she said slowly. "I'm not really supposed to grant wishes, because I don't have my final certificate."

"*Boo hoo hoooooooooo!*" Perfecta threw herself onto the floor. "I'll be the *only* princess wearing tatters and rags . . ."

"No, you won't!" Sophia snapped.

"None of us has anything special to wear!"

"Emily has! She's got the most beautiful new dress! And a sparkly new tiara!" Perfecta wailed. "Dear Fairy Angora, you seem so nice . . . please help me!"

Fairy Angora was looking very upset herself. "You poor girl," she said. "Maybe it would be all right if I granted you just a *little* wish . . ."

Of course, Perfecta stopped crying at once. She sat bolt upright. "I'd like a dress," she said. "A dress like Emily's!"

Fairy Angora's wand really was very sparkly! Much more than Fairy

G.'s. And it glowed a beautiful forget-me-not blue as she waved it.

Tingle . . . ping!

The dress was *exactly* like mine! I couldn't say anything, though, because suddenly everybody was asking for wishes. Honestly, I couldn't hear myself think!

Fairy Angora began to look a bit flustered. "Oh, dear!" she said. "I really shouldn't—I mean, I can't—"

"But it won't be fair if we don't all have wishes!" Princess Ermentrude thumped her fist on a table.

"No," Floreen whined. "It won't!"

Poor Fairy Angora grew very pale. "I'll see what I can do," she said. "Only please don't all talk at once!"

I felt very sorry for her. She looked as if she was about to burst into tears.

"Why don't we take turns?" I suggested.

Fairy Angora gulped. "Who's first?" she asked.

Floreen wanted a tiara just like mine. Lisa chose a new dress, and so did Jemima, and then everybody wanted dresses, except for Princess Nancy. She asked for a tiara decorated with silver butterflies.

Fairy Angora looked more and more anxious as the dresses piled higher and higher. I suddenly wondered if the magic was wearing out. Her wand had almost stopped sparkling and was a funny pale yellow color. Then Princess Freya's

dress came out blue instead of
pink, and Jemima had spots on her
dress instead of bows!

"Ask for something easy," I whispered when at last it was time for the Rose Room Princesses.

Charlotte asked for curly hair. Katie asked for new shoes, and

Daisy for a feather boa. Sophia asked for a silk shawl, and Alice wanted sparkly socks.

I was last, and I couldn't think of anything. Honestly, I couldn't. The only thing I really wanted was tiara points, and it would have been cheating to ask for those. In the end, I asked for a powder puff.

Fairy Angora waved her wand for the last time. One single silver sparkle floated into the air, and then—

Tingle . . . plunk!

There was my powder puff, and a pot of sparkly powder. It was so pretty!

Charlotte began to clap, and everyone joined in—even Perfecta and Floreen.

Fairy Angora looked a little bit brighter. "I do hope you enjoy your wishes," she said. "Maybe you should take your dresses and hang them up?"

At once there was a dash for the door . . . and I noticed something weird.

Do you remember that I told you Nancy wanted a tiara with butterflies on it? Well, the butterflies had turned into tiny silver caterpillars!

Chapter Three

"*Caterpillars?*" Alice stared at me as if she thought I was crazy.

"Yes," I said.

"Emily!" Daisy waved her wonderfully fluffy new feather boa under my nose. "That's such a lie!"

"They *were*," I said. "Honestly!"

Katie looked at me doubtfully, and bent down to tighten the straps on her new sparkly shoes. "I *hate* caterpillars," she said.

Sophia shook her head. "Shouldn't you save your shoes for the Grand Assembly?"

"I thought I'd wear them in." Katie stood up. "Don't they look fabulous?"

They did, but it was a good thing she'd finished fiddling with them, because just then the bell rang for Deportment Class. We had to scurry off as fast as we could because Deportment is given by Queen Gloriana, and she hates it if we're late. She gives a minus tiara point for every minute we miss! And we would have gotten there in time, but Daisy's fluffy feather boa fluttered off her neck and zoomed away all by itself down the corridor!

"Quick!" Daisy yelled. "Catch it!"

We dashed after it as fast as we could. Charlotte was about to catch it (she can run like the wind) when the *scariest* voice asked, "What *exactly* is going on?"

As Queen Gloriana swept toward us, the feather boa twitched and disappeared around a corner.

We were each given twenty minus tiara points. It was so awful. I could see Perfecta and Floreen snickering as we were sent to stand at the back of the class.

"I'm so, so sorry," Daisy whispered.

"Don't worry," Charlotte whispered back.

Queen Gloriana turned to see who was whispering. "Who—?" she began, and then she stopped. And stared.

So did *everybody*.

Charlotte's hair was growing *straight up*!

Poor Charlotte couldn't see what was going on. She put her hand to her head and gasped.

"Is this some kind of silly joke?" Queen Gloriana asked in her chilliest voice. "Because if it is, I don't think it is at *all* funny. Princess Charlotte, I expected better behavior from you. *Much* better. Take ten minus tiara points."

Charlotte burst into tears and ran out of the room.

"Please, Your Majesty," I said hurriedly. "It's not Charlotte's fault!

Truly it isn't!" And I rushed after Charlotte.

I found her in the downstairs bathroom with her head under the cold water tap. She was trying to

make her hair lie down, but it wouldn't.

"I'll have to cut it all off!" she wailed. "Oh, I wish Fairy G. were here! She'd know what to do!"

"I'll go and find Fairy Angora," I said. I zipped out of the bathroom toward Fairy G.'s office.

The Tiara Club

Princess Emily

Go to *www.tiaraclubbooks.com!*
Enter the secret word from each book. Download dazzling posters you can decorate with your Tiara Club stickers.

KATHERINE TEGEN BOOKS • *An Imprint of* HarperCollins*Publishers* • Sticker art © 2007 by PiAF

Fairy Angora opened the door the minute I knocked.

"Please!" I panted. *"Please! Charlotte's hair just won't stay down, and Daisy's feather boa is whizzing around the school, and we're in so much trouble! Please could you come and tell Queen Gloriana it isn't Charlotte's fault, and can you do something about her hair?"*

Fairy Angora looked horrified. "But I *can't!*" she said. "I don't have any magic left!" She blushed and continued. "You see, I'm still in training, so I only have one wandful of magic, and it's all gone." She went even redder. "I should never have granted you those wishes. If the Fairy God-mothers Agency ever finds out they'll send me away. Please don't tell anyone what I did!"

I couldn't believe what I was hear-ing. *Fairy Angora couldn't help us!*

My brain was whirling around and around and around, and I kept thinking, just like Charlotte, *I wish Fairy G. were here!*

Then I had a totally brilliant idea. "What would happen," I asked, "if we gave our wishes back? What if we gave back all the dresses and tiaras and my powder puff and everything? Would you be able to get the magic back into your wand?"

Fairy Angora stared at me. Then she nodded. "Yes," she said. "At least, I think so."

I didn't know how to explain the next part of my idea without sounding rude, so I just had to say it.

"If you *can* get the magic back, would there be enough for one big wish? Could I wish that Fairy G. was all better, and back here at the Princess Academy?"

I'd thought Fairy Angora would be offended, but she wasn't. She gave a little sigh instead. "Emily," she said, "I wish you'd thought of that before."

"Me too," I said—and I really really, *really* meant it.

Chapter Four

That was the easy part. The problem was how to get all the first-year princesses to give up their lovely dresses . . . especially Perfecta and Floreen!

Charlotte, Alice, Katie, Daisy, and Sophia did their best to help, but it took us forever. Luckily nearly everyone loves Fairy G. When we explained we needed the dresses to get the magic back so Fairy Angora could make her better, they sighed a little, then stomped off to get them. Nancy was more than happy to give us back her caterpillar tiara. She said it was creepy.

But we were left with three huge problems, and we didn't know what to do.

Perfecta absolutely *wouldn't* give up her dress.

Floreen totally *wouldn't* give up her tiara.

And we kept getting minus tiara points.

Charlotte's hair settled down, but Daisy's feather boa kept popping up

in the most awkward places. She got more and more minus tiara points for untidiness until *finally* Daisy caught it—but then Queen Mother Matilda gave Daisy five minus tiara points for running in the hallway.

Sophia woke up to find her shawl had vanished. Guess where it was? In the kitchen. Cook Clara said

Sophia must have been playing in the kitchen, and gave her three minus tiara points.

Katie's shoes danced away on

their own the moment she took them off, and King Percival tripped over them. Eight minus tiara points for Katie!

Alice's sparkly socks made her feet itch, and she got six minus tiara points for scratching in class.

We were desperate. We just *had* to get Fairy G. back . . . but how?

"At least we'll all be repeating the first year together," Charlotte said gloomily. "The Grand Assembly is tomorrow, and we must have many more minus tiara points than plus ones."

"No!" I said. "We'll get Fairy G. back, and she'll figure it out. Let's go and see Fairy Angora after tea. We'll bring her the dresses and Nancy's tiara and our things. Maybe that'll be enough to refill the wand."

But it wasn't. Fairy Angora waved her wand over the dresses and the

tiara and the wriggling boa . . . but
nothing happened.

No sparkles. Nothing. And the
wand stayed a nasty yellow.

"We need *everything*," she said
sadly. "I think the magic must have
been at its strongest when I wished
for Perfecta's dress and Floreen's
tiara."

"Oh," I said.

"I'm so sorry." Fairy Angora put her wand down and looked at us.

"Do you miss Fairy G. very much?"

We nodded.

"It's actually not so bad to repeat the first year—lots of princesses do. But that's not the most important thing," Katie said.

"That's right," Alice agreed. "We just want Fairy G. back!"

And that was when I had the best idea I'd ever *ever* had.

Suddenly, I knew exactly how I could persuade Perfecta and Floreen to give up the dress and the tiara! I swallowed and tried to ignore the fluttery feelings in my stomach.

"Excuse me!" I said. "I won't be long!" And I hurried out of Fairy G.'s study.

"I've done it!" I yelled as I zoomed back through the door, the dress

over my arm and the tiara clutched
safely in my hand.

Sophia leaped to her feet.

"Emily!" she said. "You *didn't*
give Perfecta your beautiful birthday dress!"

I nodded, trying to look as if I
didn't care one teeny tiny bit.

"It was the only way," I said.

"And I gave Floreen my tiara. It doesn't matter—honestly! Besides, I want to wear an old dress for the Grand Assembly, just like all of you."

"Oh, Emily!" Charlotte said, and she hugged me.

"And now can you try again to get your magic back?" I asked Fairy Angora.

She nodded as she looked at the pile of dresses and things on the floor. Then she bit her lip and waved her wand.

"Oh, my magic wishes," she whispered. "Please—*be gone!*"

There was a gigantic flash, and we all jumped.

The floor was clear—*and Fairy Angora's wand was bright blue!*

"Wow!" we all said at the same time.

Daisy whispered, *"Magic!"*

I looked anxiously at Fairy

Angora. "Please!" I begged. "Please wish for Fairy G. to be better! Please have her come back right now this minute!"

Fairy Angora smiled and waved her wand again. We held our breath.

There was a tinkling of silver bells, and for a moment the whole room was full of dancing, shimmering silver sparkles . . . but nothing else. And Fairy Angora's wand was back to that awful nasty yellow.

"Oh, dear," she said sadly. "It didn't work."

We dragged ourselves out of Fairy G.'s study.

Chapter Five

I don't think we'd ever felt as terrible as we did on the morning of the Grand Assembly. It was supposed to be the most glorious day of the whole school year, but for us it was the worst. All the other princesses were furious with us, and I could see why.

We'd taken away their truly glorious dresses—and Fairy G. still wasn't back!

And we had lots and lots and *lots* of minus tiara points.

We held hands as we trailed miserably down the stairs.

The Great Hall was packed. I've *never* seen so many kings and queens and princes and princesses all in one place.

There was a burst of trumpets as Queen Gloriana sailed onto the stage to join Queen Mother

Matilda, Lady Victoria, King Percival, and all the other teachers who work at the Academy.

Everyone was there—except Fairy G.

"I am very pleased to welcome you all to our special ceremony," Queen Gloriana announced. "We have had another excellent year, and I am happy to say that many of our princesses have earned a splendid number of tiara points. Some, alas, have *not* done so well."

I felt Charlotte squeeze my hand. I tried to smile at her, but I couldn't. I blinked to stop myself from crying, but a tear trickled down my nose.

Queen Gloriana was still talking. "Now, I am truly delighted to welcome a *very* special guest. She will award all the tiara points, and she has the names of the princesses who have earned their places in the Tiara Club!"

There was another fanfare of trumpets . . . and my mouth dropped wide open.

Fairy G.—bigger and better than I'd ever seen her—was floating down onto the stage in a twinkly pink cloud of fairy dust. She landed with a solid *thump!* and beamed at us.

"I'm so pleased to be here!" she boomed.

"I would not have been able to attend, however, had it not been for the efforts of six very special princesses—the Princesses Emily, Alice, Charlotte, Katie, Daisy, and Sophia! And I wish to award them one hundred tiara points each, as a mark of my appreciation!"

Tantara! Tantara! Tantara! went the trumpets—and the six of us stood and stared at one another. My heart was pitter-pattering so loudly I couldn't breathe, and a sudden wild and fantastical hope zoomed into my head!

I hardly dared to think it—*could that mean we had enough tiara points?* Numbers skittered in and out of my brain. Was a hundred enough? I didn't know! Oh, if *only* I'd counted my points, if only I'd written them down—if only, if *only*!

Tantara! Tantara! Tantara! went the trumpets again, and my stomach fluttered with a million butterflies as I watched Fairy G. hand a silver envelope to Queen Gloriana.

It seemed like a hundred thousand years before Queen Gloriana pulled out the paper inside.

"Ahem," she said. "I have much pleasure in welcoming the following princesses to the Tiara Club: Princess Alice"—and Alice squeaked!

She really did!—"Princess Daisy,
Princess Sophia, Princess Katie,
Princess Charlotte, and—"

Queen Gloriana paused for a
second, and I nearly died—

"And, of course, Princess Emily!"

I didn't know what to do.

Nor did any of my friends.

We were stunned!

Then Charlotte dug her elbow into me. *"Look!"* she whispered.

A deep rose-red carpet was rolling across the floor of the Great Hall, and it stopped right in front of us. We stepped onto it. Pale pink rose petals fluttered down, and I'm sure I could hear the sounds of birds singing as the golden trumpets sang out yet again.

As we proceeded up the rose-red carpet toward the waiting Queen Gloriana and Fairy G., I suddenly realized we were *all* dressed in the

most beautiful satin gowns.

We reached Queen Gloriana, and we curtsied . . . perfectly.

"Welcome, princesses," Queen

Gloriana said. "Welcome to the Tiara Club!"

I nearly burst with pride as I took my tiara—the tiara that meant I was a Perfect Princess, and a member of the Tiara Club!

Princess Emily
The Tiara Club
The Silver Towers
The Royal Palace Academy
for the Preparation of
Perfect Princesses

Dear Princess Emily,

I PASSED! And now I'm a REAL Fairy Godmother. Thank you for everything you taught me. One day I hope some princesses will love me as much as you love Fairy G.

All VERY best wishes,

Fairy GODMOTHER
Angora xxx

P.S. I'll see you next term . . . in the Silver Towers!

What happens next?

FIND OUT IN

Princess Charlotte
∾ AND THE ∾
Enchanted Rose

Good day, dear Tiara Club Princess. Princess Charlotte sends you greetings!

Oh, it's no good. I don't think I'll ever be able to talk like a real princess. But I'm so pleased you're coming to Silver Towers at the Royal Palace Academy with me and Katie, Daisy, Alice, Sophia, and Emily—it'll be such fun! We'll float around being Perfect Princesses, and every day will be just perfect . . . although my first day wasn't perfect at all!

You are cordially invited to visit www.tiaraclubbooks.com!

Visit your special princess friends at their dazzling website!

Find the secret word hidden in each of the first six Tiara Club books. Then go to the Tiara Club website, enter the secret word, and get an exclusive poster. Print out the poster for each book and save it. When you have all six, put them together to make one amazing poster of the entire Royal Princess Academy. Use the stickers in the books to decorate and make your very own perfect princess academy poster.

More fun at www.tiaraclubbooks.com:

• Download your own Tiara Club membership card!

• Win future Tiara Club books.

• Get activities and coloring sheets with every new book.

• Stay up-to-date with the princesses in this great series!

Visit www.tiaraclubbooks.com and be a part of the Tiara Club!